Published in 2018
by Autumn Publishing
Cottage Farm
Sywell
NN6 0BJ
www.igloobooks.com

"101 Dalmatians" is based on the book *The Hundred and One Dalmatians* by Dodie Smith, published by The Viking Press.

"The Aristocats" is based on the book by Thomas Rowe.

"The Jungle Book" is based on the Mowgli Stories in *The Jungle Book* and *The Second Jungle Book* by Rudyard Kipling.

"Peter Pan" was adapted by Lisa McClatchy.

"The Jungle Book" was adapted by Elizabeth Rudnick.

"Aladdin", "The Aristocats", "Lady and the Tramp" and "The Lion King"
were adapted by Satia Stevens.

"101 Dalmatians", "Bambi" and "Pinocchio," were adapted by Kelsey Skea.

Illustrations by the Disney Storybook Artists

TOP002 0818
2 4 6 8 10 9 7 5 3 1
ISBN 978-1-78810-270-4

Printed and manufactured in China

DISNEP
STORYBOOK
COLLECTION

Autumn
Publishing

Contents

One spring morning, the animals of the forest woke to an exciting event. Bluebirds soared through the sky chirping the news to quails, squirrels, chipmunks and beavers.

A small bunny named Thumper heard what had happened. He hopped to see Friend Owl, who was sleeping.

"Wake up!" the bunny cried, thumping his foot excitedly. "The new prince is born!"

Thumper and Friend Owl went to a small thicket. There, next to a proud doe, lay a newborn fawn. He was the new Prince of the Forest, and all the animals had come to see him. The little prince tried to stand up. But his legs were wobbly and he fell right back down.

Thumper giggled. "Whatcha gonna call him?" he asked.

"I think I'll call him Bambi," the mama deer said, as she nuzzled her son.

Soon, Bambi and his mother went for their first walk together. Bambi met many of the forest animals along the way. First, Mrs Quail and her babies stopped to say hello.

Then, Mrs Opossum and her family, who liked to hang upside down from a tree, greeted him. Next, a mole poked his head out of the ground to wish Bambi a good day.

Later, Bambi tried to scamper and slipped on a reed. "He doesn't walk very good, does he?" Thumper said.

"What did your father tell you this morning?" Thumper's mother asked him sternly.

"If you can't say something nice," the bunny replied, guiltily, "don't say nothing at all."

The bunny and his sisters ran over to help Bambi up. Then they began to play together, showing him how to hop over a log.

When they pointed out some bluebirds, Bambi tried to speak. "Bur-duh," he said slowly. With a little practise, it got easier. "Bird, bird, bird, bird!" Bambi cried.

Bambi and Thumper continued to explore the forest. A yellow butterfly landed on the fawn's tail. Bambi was fascinated with it and soon learnt how to say 'butterfly'. When it flew to a brightly coloured flower patch, Bambi and Thumper followed.

Thumper taught his new friend the word, 'flower'. Bambi was smelling the flowers when he found himself nose to nose with a skunk who had been doing the same thing.

"Flower!" Bambi said, proudly, when he saw the skunk. Thumper laughed. "That's not a flower. He's a little—"

The skunk interrupted. "Oh, that's alright. He can call me a flower if he wants to." He giggled, bashfully. Bambi, Thumper and Flower became great friends.

One day, Bambi's mother took him to the meadow for the first time. The fawn was very excited. He hoped he might meet other deer there. At the edge of the forest, Bambi saw the grassy meadow and bounded forwards. His mother leapt in front of him.

"You must never rush out on the meadow," she warned. "The meadow is wide and open, and there are no trees or bushes to hide us, so we have to be very careful."

Once Bambi's mother told him it was safe, the young deer hurried into the soft grass, eager to play in the wide-open space. He had never been anywhere like this before.

Bambi followed a frog and came to a pond. He stopped at the water and saw his reflection. He thought it was another deer, but everywhere he moved, it moved. Finally, he realised it wasn't another deer. It was a reflection of him! Then, he saw a different image in the water and heard a giggle. A girl fawn named Faline had come to the pond. She had blue eyes and was very pretty.

As Faline got closer, Bambi ran away and hid between his mother's legs.

"He's kinda bashful, isn't he, mama?" Faline asked her mother. Faline said hello a couple of times and finally Bambi replied.

Soon, the two deer were frolicking in the woods. They played tag and became fast friends.

While Bambi and Faline were playing, a herd of stags galloped by. One was larger than all the rest and the other animals in the forest stopped what they were doing to look at him.

The stag stood still for a moment and stared at Bambi. The young prince didn't know the stag was his father. "He's very brave and very wise," Bambi's mother explained to her son. "That's why he's known as the Great Prince of the Forest."

Just then, the sound of a gunshot rang out.

The animals all rushed to safety, but Bambi got separated from his mother.

Luckily, the Great Prince guided him towards the thicket. Partway there, Bambi's mother joined them. When they'd made it to safety, the Great Prince left.

Time passed and soon it was Bambi's first winter.

One day, he went to the pond with Thumper, who glided across its icy surface. "Look, the water's stiff!" Thumper exclaimed.

Bambi leapt onto the ice and fell flat on his stomach. Thumper laughed. He showed his friend how to stand up and slide across.

Winter was fun at first, but after a while Bambi longed for the warmth of spring. He was hungry and some of his friends, including Flower, slept all winter long. He missed them.

One afternoon, Bambi and his mother were in the forest. He was very excited because he'd found a small patch of grass. It looked like a feast. But in the distance, a shot rang out. Man was in the forest again, hunting.

He and his mother ran towards the thicket. "Faster, Bambi!" she urged. Just as he reached home, Bambi heard a second shot and noticed his mother wasn't with him anymore. He looked and looked, then realised he was all alone.

Bambi began to cry. Soon the Great Prince came to him. "Your mother can't be with you anymore," his father said.

"Man has taken her away. Now you must be brave and learn to walk alone."

Bambi lowered his head, sadly.

"Come, my son," the Great Prince said. Bambi followed his father into the forest.

A couple of months later, spring arrived. Over the winter, Bambi had grown into a handsome young stag with antlers. His friends Thumper and Flower had grown up, too. Before long, Flower met a pretty skunk and fell in love. Then, Thumper met a beautiful bunny and also fell in love.

Bambi didn't understand what had happened to his friends until he ran into Faline again. She had grown into a gorgeous doe. Bambi suddenly felt a little dizzy, but very, very happy. He and Faline were in love.

One day, a stag appeared and challenged him for Faline's love. The two deer fought. Bambi butted the stag with all his might. After a long battle, the newcomer finally limped off. Bambi had won! From that day on, he and Faline were always together.

Spring turned into summer, which faded into autumn. One morning, Bambi smelt something strange – smoke. It was from a campfire.

Just then a majestic stag appeared. It was Bambi's father, the Great Prince. "It's Man," he said. "We must go deep into the forest – hurry!"

Fear spread through the forest. Thumper and his family hid in their burrows. Flower and his family went underground. The beavers dived underwater and the squirrels climbed high into the trees. Bambi and Faline ran, but soon a pack of dogs surrounded Faline. Bambi fought off the dogs and Faline ran to safety. But a hunter shot Bambi and he fell to the ground.

In the meantime, the forest had caught fire. The Great Prince came and urged Bambi to get up. The young prince used all the strength he had and followed his father to an island in the river, where the rest of the animals were waiting.

They stayed there until the fire died down.

Autumn once again turned into winter and winter into spring. The forest was lush and green and smelt of blooming flowers.

Soon, Thumper and his little bunnies were waking Friend Owl again. Faline had given birth to twin fawns. All the animals came to celebrate.

But no one was prouder than Bambi, the new Prince of the Forest. He stood overlooking the thicket with his father, smiling down on his family, his heart filled with love. Bambi knew he would teach his children the lessons of the forest that he had learnt.

THE LION KING

Everything in the animal kingdom had its place in the circle of life. When the Lion King of the Pride Lands, Mufasa, and his queen, Sarabi, had a cub named Simba, Mufasa knew that one day his son would be king. All the animals bowed in respect as the wise baboon shaman, Rafiki, introduced the young prince.

Simba grew into a healthy and energetic cub. One day, after an outing with his father, he wandered into the cave of his uncle, Scar. Until Simba was born, Mufasa's brother had been next in line for the throne. Scar was jealous of Simba, but the cub didn't know that.

Simba proudly told his uncle, "My dad just showed me the whole kingdom. And I'm gonna rule it all."

"He didn't show you what's beyond that rise at the northern border," Scar said, slyly.

"He said I can't go," Simba replied.

"He's absolutely right. Only the bravest lions go there," Scar said, to tempt his nephew. "An elephant graveyard is no place for a young prince."

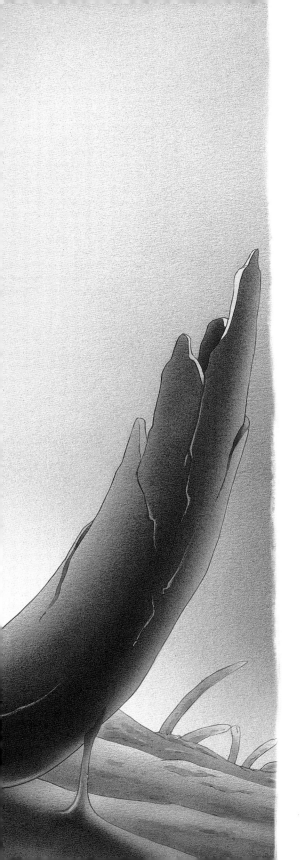

Simba immediately raced home and convinced Nala, a girl cub who was his best friend, to explore the Elephant Graveyard with him.

When they got there, the cubs looked at the elephant bones with awe. They were just about to step inside a giant skull when Zazu, a bird who was the king's adviser, caught up to warn them how dangerous it was outside the Pride Lands.

"Danger? Ha! I walk on the wild side," Simba said, confidently. "I laugh in the face of danger."

Just then, Simba turned to see three large hyenas who looked very hungry.

"Do you know what we do to kings who step out of their kingdom?" one hyena threatened.

Then, the snarling hyenas chased the cubs into a ravine that was blocked by a large elephant skeleton.

The cubs were trapped! Suddenly, there was a tremendous roar. Mufasa arrived and frightened the hyenas away.

Zazu took Nala home. Mufasa scolded his son for putting her in danger.

Simba was ashamed that he had disobeyed his father. "I was just trying to be brave like you," he said, sadly.

"I'm only brave when I have to be," Mufasa said. "Being brave doesn't mean you go looking for trouble."

"I guess even kings get scared, huh?" Simba asked.

Mufasa nodded gravely at the young cub. Father and son rested in the tall grass and gazed at the evening sky. Simba loved spending time with his father. "We'll always be together, right?" he asked.

"Look at the stars," said Mufasa. "The great kings of the past look down on us from those stars. Remember that those kings will always be there to guide you. So will I."

When Scar heard that Simba had escaped, he made a plan with the hyenas. One day, Scar brought his nephew into a gorge and promised him a wonderful surprise if he would wait on a certain rock. Then, on Scar's signal, the hyenas chased a herd of wildebeests until they began a furious stampede!

As the wildebeests headed towards him, Simba climbed up a tree. He held on tight, but he was slipping fast. He didn't know how much longer he could hang on.

Suddenly, Mufasa appeared and carried Simba to a ledge. But a wildebeest slammed into Mufasa, knocking him into the thundering stampede.

"Daaaad!" Simba cried.

Mufasa leapt up and clung to the edge of a cliff, trying to pull himself to safety. By the time Simba got there, it was too late. His father had died.

Simba had not seen Scar push his father, so believed Mufasa's death was his fault.

"Run away, Simba," Scar advised the young cub. "Run away and never return."

The hyenas chased the young cub far away. Then Scar returned to Pride Rock and announced to the lions that he would be their new king.

Simba ran until he collapsed in the desert from heat and exhaustion. Luckily, two curious animals found him – a meerkat called Timon and a warthog named Pumbaa.

Simba's new friends took him home to the jungle and introduced him to a fun-loving way of life. Timon liked to say hakuna matata a lot, which meant 'no worries'.

Even when he had his doubts, Simba tried grubs and other unusual foods that his new friends said were delicious. He played in the waterfalls and gazed at the stars with Timon and Pumbaa.

It was fun, but Simba often thought about his family and his old life. He did his best to put the past behind him.

The years passed and Simba grew up. One day, a young lioness came to the jungle looking for food. Simba recognised her. It was Nala, his best friend from when he was a cub. She told him what had happened since Scar had taken over the Pride Lands. The hyenas roamed freely and there was no food or water for anyone. Nala believed that Simba was the only one who could save them.

"We've really needed you at home," Nala said. "You're the king. If you don't do something soon, everyone will starve."

Simba was heartbroken, but he could not face going back. Then, Rafiki appeared. The wise baboon convinced Simba to forget his doubts.

"You follow old Rafiki. He knows the way."

The shaman led Simba through the jungle. They stopped beside a pool of water, then Simba looked up. A vision of his father appeared in the night sky.

"You must take your place in the circle of life," Mufasa advised. "You are my son and the one true king."

Simba knew his father was right.

With his friends by his side, Simba returned to Pride Rock.

In front of all the animals, he confronted Scar.

"The choice is yours. Either step down or fight," Simba challenged.

Scar refused to give up his throne. Instead, he told everyone that Simba was responsible for Mufasa's death. He cornered his nephew on a cliff. Suddenly, Simba's foot slipped and he was hanging from the edge, just as his father had.

Scar leant over. "Here's my little secret," he whispered. "I killed Mufasa."

At last, Simba found the strength to fight back. He leapt up over the cliff edge and tackled his uncle. He forced Scar to admit that he was responsible for Mufasa's death. Hearing the truth, the lion pride defended Simba against the hyenas.

Simba and Scar battled across Pride Rock, exchanging powerful blows. Finally, they both fell near the edge. Simba ordered his uncle to leave the Pride Lands. But Scar attacked Simba again.

Simba dodged the blow and Scar fell over the side of the cliff.

When the fighting was over, Simba took his rightful place as the Lion King and restored the Pride Lands to a place of peace and beauty. Simba and Nala found happiness together and when their little cub was born, a new circle of life began.

On a quiet street in London lived a family named the Darlings. Mr and Mrs Darling had three children – Wendy, John and Michael. All three played and slept in the nursery.

Wendy was the oldest. Each night before bed, she told her brothers all about the adventures of a hero named Peter Pan.

John and Michael loved those stories. They romped through the house, pretending to have sword fights with pirates and look for treasure, just like Peter Pan.

One night, Mr Darling was getting ready to go out with his wife. He was quite frantic because his gold cuff links were missing and Michael had drawn a treasure map on his last clean shirt. Mr Darling blamed Wendy for filling the boys' heads with stories of Peter Pan.

He decided that night would be Wendy's last in the nursery. He thought she was ready to have a room of her own. Wendy was shocked. The boys were, too.

"Sooner or later, people have to grow up," Mr Darling said.

Mrs Darling tucked the children up in bed, and before long, they were fast asleep.

Later that night, Peter Pan and a fairy named Tinker Bell flew into the nursery. Peter often listened outside the window while Wendy told stories about him. The last time he was there, he'd lost his shadow and he needed it back.

Soon, he found the shadow, but it tried to escape. Luckily, Wendy woke up and insisted upon sewing it back on. She told Peter that it was her last night in the nursery, for tomorrow she would have to grow up.

"No, I won't have it!" cried Peter. "Come on!"

"But where are we going?" asked Wendy.

"Never Land," he replied. "You'll never grow up there."

With all the commotion, John and Michael woke up. Peter Pan agreed that they could come along, too.

After a sprinkling of pixie dust, the Darling children rose into the air and followed Peter and Tinker Bell out the window.

"We can fly!" they shouted, as they flew over the city.

Meanwhile, in Never Land, a pirate named Captain Hook was busy scheming with his first mate, Mr Smee. Hook wanted revenge against Peter Pan. Long ago, Peter had chopped off Hook's hand in a sword fight and thrown it to a crocodile to eat. The Crocodile thought it was delicious and now he followed the pirate everywhere, hoping for another bite. Hook was constantly on the lookout for the hungry animal.

Hook didn't know where to find Peter, so he decided to kidnap Tiger Lily, the Indian Chief's daughter. She was a good friend of Peter Pan's and Hook was sure they could get her to reveal the location of his hideout.

As Peter, Tinker Bell and the children approached Never Land, Peter shouted, "There it is, Wendy!" and pointed to the wondrous land below.

"Oh, Peter, it's just as I've always dreamt it would be!" Wendy replied, excitedly. But Captain Hook had spotted Peter Pan flying in the clouds.

He shot a cannonball towards them. Peter and the children jumped behind a cloud. Luckily, it zoomed by and they didn't get hurt.

"Quick, Tink! Take Wendy and the boys to the island!" yelled Peter, as he raced down towards Hook's ship.

While Peter distracted Hook, Tinker Bell hurried towards the island. She flew so fast that Wendy, John and Michael fell far behind. The fairy thought Peter Pan was spending too much time with Wendy. She was jealous, so she went to see the Lost Boys, who lived with Peter in Hangman's Tree. Peter was their leader – they'd do anything he said.

So Tink told them that Peter wanted them to shoot the Wendy bird out of the sky.

The Lost Boys grabbed their slingshots and aimed at Wendy. Fortunately, Peter arrived in time to save her as she fell towards the ground. He was very angry with Tinker Bell, though.

"Tinker Bell, I hereby banish you forever!" he shouted.

"Please, not forever," Wendy pleaded. She and her brothers were fine, after all.

"Well, for a week then," Peter agreed. But Tink didn't hear him. She had already flown away.

Next, Peter took Wendy on a tour of Never Land. While visiting the mermaids, Peter spotted Hook interrogating Tiger Lily, who was tied to a rock in the water. The pirate was still convinced she knew the location of Peter's hiding place. But Tiger Lily wouldn't give him any information.

Peter revealed himself and challenged Hook. They fought one another, and as they did, the rising tide got closer and closer to Tiger Lily's head. Peter Pan finally won, sending Hook into the water, where the Crocodile was waiting. The pirate swam away quickly and Smee rowed out to save him.

Peter swooped down and rescued Tiger Lily just as the water was about to cover her. He brought her safely back to her village. Her father, the Chief, named Peter 'Eagle Feathers' and there was a great celebration.

The only one who didn't celebrate was Tinker Bell. She still thought Peter had banished her forever and was very upset. Captain Hook had heard what had happened and he sent Smee to fetch her immediately. Hook persuaded Tink to tell him that Hangman's Tree was the entrance to Peter's hiding place. But before she did, she made him promise not to harm Peter.

Later, while Peter was out, Hook's pirates went to his hideout and kidnapped Wendy, John, Michael and the Lost Boys. Hook left a bomb (disguised as a present!) for Peter. Then, he took the children back to his ship and tied them up.

They didn't know how they would ever escape.

Tinker Bell was shocked when she discovered Hook's plans to blow up Peter. With only minutes to spare, she flew as fast as she could to warn him. Peter was about to unwrap the present, but Tink grabbed it right before it exploded. KABOOM!

Peter didn't think Tinker Bell had survived the blast. He was upset, but he didn't want anyone else to get hurt, so he raced back to Hook's ship to save the children. When he got there, Wendy was walking the plank!

Peter caught her right before she fell into the water.

Then, he jumped on the ship's deck and challenged Hook. "This time you've gone too far!" he yelled. Just then, Tinker Bell flew by. She had survived!

"You wouldn't dare fight old Hook man-to-man," the pirate sneered.

"I'll fight you man-to-man with one hand behind my back!" countered Peter. They began to duel. Meanwhile, John, Michael and the Lost Boys climbed to the crow's nest and battled the other pirates. The Lost Boys threw rocks and fired slingshots as the pirates got close to them. One by one, the pirates were defeated – all except Hook, who was still fighting Peter.

Peter and Hook battled it out on the ship's yardarm, which had swung over the water. Peter grabbed Hook's sword, but then decided to let him go. However, the pirate had been humiliated. He took a swipe at Peter, lost his balance and plunged into the water – right into the jaws of the Crocodile. "Smee!" Hook cried, as the ferocious Crocodile chased him far out to sea. "Cap'n, wait for us!" his first mate yelled, as he and the pirates rowed after Hook in a small lifeboat.

Peter took control of Hook's ship and Wendy and the rest of the children cheered. "Hooray for Captain Pan!"

"Could you tell me, sir, where we're sailing?" asked Wendy with a smile.

"To London, Madam," replied Peter.

"Michael, John… we're going home!" cried Wendy, joyfully. The children were all very happy for they had grown homesick.

Tinker Bell sprinkled the ship with pixie dust and soon it was flying out of the water, through the air and back to London.

Below them, Never Land grew smaller and smaller until it finally disappeared. Wendy and her brothers said goodbye to Peter. They knew they would always remember their marvellous adventure.

At home, Wendy told her parents she was ready to grow up. Then they gazed out the window together, just in time to see the ship pass across the moon.

"You know," Mr Darling said, his arm round his daughter, "I have the strangest feeling that I've seen that ship before… a long time ago."

Long ago, a kind old woman named Madame Bonfamille lived in a beautiful house in Paris. She had a cat named Duchess, who had three kittens named Toulouse, Berlioz and Marie. The kittens were very talented. Toulouse could paint and Berlioz could play the piano. Marie, who had white fur like her mother, liked to sing.

Madame loved Duchess and her kittens very much. She even made plans to leave her entire fortune to them. But when her butler, Edgar, found out, he was very upset.

He had been taking care of Madame and her cats for years and had always thought he would inherit her fortune.

Edgar decided to make the cats disappear, so Madame would leave her money to him instead.

That evening, Edgar put something in the cats' supper that would make them very sleepy. "Come taste this delicious crème de la crème à la Edgar!" he called, as he put down their food. The cats and their mouse friend Roquefort ate it all up. Roquefort went to his mouse hole to rest and the cats fell asleep. Edgar put the cats in a basket and drove them out to the country. Along the way, two noisy dogs started to chase them.

Edgar lost control of his motorcycle and drove into a river.

The basket holding the cats fell off the motorcycle and rolled under a bridge.

Edgar couldn't find it, so he returned to Paris.

When he got home, Roquefort had woken up. The mouse began to suspect that Edgar was behind the cats' disappearance.

When Duchess and her kittens woke up, they were in the dark countryside.

They didn't know how they had got there or how to get home. It was raining, so they huddled together to stay warm.

Luckily, the next morning, an alley cat named Thomas O'Malley found the kittens and their mother at the bridge.

He knew the journey back to Paris would be difficult for the little ones, so he offered to help.

O'Malley sneaked the family on to a milk lorry. As the lorry began to move, Marie fell off the back. The alley cat rescued her and hopped aboard. The cats drank some of the cream on the lorry, but when the driver discovered them, he chased the cats away.

When they got to O'Malley's place, some of his friends were there singing and playing jazz. The leader of the jazz band stepped forwards and O'Malley introduced him as Scat Cat. He was the coolest cat on the Parisian jazz scene and he could play the trumpet and sing better than anyone.

The cats had never heard jazz before, but soon all the kittens were dancing. Then, O'Malley asked Duchess to dance. The band played one jazz tune after another and before long it was very late.

The kittens were still humming when their mother put them to bed. They had never had so much fun.

After a very long walk, a bridge crossing and an accidental tumble into a river, the cats finally reached Paris late at night. O'Malley had stayed with Duchess and her kittens the entire time.

Berlioz, Toulouse and Marie were very tired from the journey. O'Malley decided they needed a rest before they went home. He led them across the rooftops to his house.

Then, O'Malley and Duchess went out to the roof and looked at the starry sky. They'd had a wonderful evening together. O'Malley knew he was in love with Duchess and he asked her to stay.

"Oh, Thomas, that would be wonderful," she said.

Duchess loved O'Malley very much and knew her kittens did, too, but she also knew she could never leave Madame.

"You're just her house pets," O'Malley protested.

"Oh no," Duchess said. "We mean far more to her than that."

"I'm gonna miss you…" O'Malley said. "And those kids."

The next day, O'Malley reluctantly took his new friends home. At the front door, they said their goodbyes and Duchess and the kittens went inside.

Edgar was mad that the cats had returned, so he put them inside a sack and hid them inside a huge trunk to be sent far away to Timbuktu.

But Roquefort had been keeping an eye on Edgar. When he saw what had happened, he ran down the street to catch up with O'Malley. Luckily, the cat hadn't got too far.

"Duchess… kittens… in trouble!" cried the little mouse. O'Malley stopped and listened, then came up with a plan to help the cats.

O'Malley sent Roquefort to get Scat Cat and his friends and bring them to Madame's. Then, he ran into the house to help Duchess. He chased Edgar into the barn and cornered him. O'Malley jumped on the butler's back, but Edgar shook the cat off. When O'Malley tried to get to the trunk to free the cats, Edgar fought him with a pitchfork!

Suddenly, Scat Cat and the gang were at the barn door. They managed to overpower the butler. Roquefort opened the trunk and O'Malley let Duchess and the kittens out.

Then, they made Edgar get into the trunk. A few minutes later, some men came to pick it up.

Finally, Edgar was gone – heading for Timbuktu.

Duchess and the kittens had a
joyful reunion with Madame. She
was delighted her precious pets
were safely home and very grateful to
Thomas O'Malley and his friends.

Madame could see that O'Malley
and Duchess were in love, so she
invited the alley cat to live with them.

Duchess and the kittens were very
happy because now their family was
complete.

Disney

THE JUNGLE BOOK

Long ago, deep in the jungles of India, there lived a wise black panther named Bagheera. One day, as Bagheera walked along the river, he saw something surprising – a baby! It was lying in a boat that had crashed onto shore. "Why, it's a Man-cub!" the panther said to himself.

Bagheera took the child to the den of a nearby wolf family. The mother had just had pups and Bagheera hoped she would take care of the Man-cub. The panther placed the baby near the den and stepped away. After a few quick sniffs, the mother wolf accepted the boy and named him Mowgli.

For ten years, Mowgli lived with the wolves and was very happy. He loved his family and he was a favourite among the other jungle animals.

But there was one jungle creature who did not like Mowgli.

It was Shere Khan, a strong and cunning tiger. He had just returned to that part of the jungle. Shere Khan feared nothing but Man's gun and Man's fire. He had heard of the young Man-cub and believed that Mowgli would grow up to be a hunter. Shere Khan wanted to make sure that did not happen.

One night, the wolf elders met at Council Rock to discuss the tiger's return. "He will surely kill the boy," Akela, the wolf leader, told the council. Then, he announced that Mowgli would have to leave the jungle.

When Bagheera heard the decision, he offered to help. "I know a Man-village where he'll be safe," he told the wolves.

"So be it," Akela said. "There is no time to lose."

Bagheera and Mowgli began their journey.

"We'll spend the night here," the panther said after a while. The pair settled down to sleep on a tree branch. They were both very tired and drifted off to sleep quickly.

Just then, Kaa the snake appeared. He thought Mowgli would make a tasty treat. Using his hypnotic eyes, Kaa put Mowgli in a trance. Then, he wrapped the Man-cub in his coils.

Bagheera woke up and saw what was happening. He quickly jumped up and hit the snake on the head. SMACK!

With a bruised head and an empty belly, Kaa slithered away. Mowgli was safe – for now.

The next morning, Mowgli and Bagheera were woken up
by loud rumbling and shaking. "A parade!" Mowgli shouted.
He swung down from the tree to get a better look.

It was a parade of elephants! Colonel Hathi, their leader,
was in front, giving orders and keeping everyone in line.

Mowgli wanted to march, too. He saw a baby elephant
and ran over to join him. Now Mowgli was really having fun!
But soon Colonel Hathi made them stop and line up for inspection.
When he saw Mowgli, he asked, "What happened to your trunk?"
Then, he realised that Mowgli wasn't an elephant. "A Man-cub!" he cried.

Bagheera came to Mowgli's rescue. "The Man-cub is with me," he told the Colonel. "I'm taking him back to his village." When Hathi heard this, he calmed down and began to march again.

After the elephants left, Bagheera told Mowgli they had to keep moving. But the Man-cub was having fun and didn't want to leave the jungle. "Then from now on, you're on your own!" the panther told him.

Mowgli walked off and soon met a fun-loving bear named Baloo.

They played together, sang together and ate bananas and coconuts all day long.

Later, the two new friends floated down the river. Suddenly, a group of monkeys swooped down and picked Mowgli up. "Give me back my Man-cub!" shouted Baloo. But the monkeys ignored the bear and carried Mowgli to their leader, King Louie.

King Louie wanted to learn how to make fire, and he thought the Man-cub
could teach him. Mowgli didn't know anything about making
fire, though. He could not help Louie and
that made the king very angry.

In the meantime, Baloo
found Bagheera.

They searched for Mowgli
and arrived just in time to
save the Man-cub.

Baloo disguised
himself as an ape
and started dancing
with Louie. Soon, all
the monkeys were dancing.

But when Baloo's
costume fell off, the monkeys
realised they'd been tricked. Baloo, Bagheera and Mowgli quickly ran
away to safety.

Later that night, Bagheera tried to convince Mowgli that the jungle was too dangerous for a young Man-cub. But Mowgli still didn't believe him and he ran away again – right into Kaa!

The snake was just about to make Mowgli into a snack when Shere Khan interrupted.

While Kaa and the tiger talked, Mowgli escaped and ran deep into the jungle.

Mowgli was finally all alone, but he was sad and tired. The Man-cub sat down on a rock to rest. Soon, four vultures flew down and started to tease him. But when they saw how lonely he was, they decided to be nicer. Just then, Shere Khan appeared. The vultures got scared and flew away quickly!

But Mowgli did not move. "You don't scare me, Shere Khan!" he said, bravely.

Shere Khan lunged at the Man-cub, his razor-sharp claws flashing. But Baloo, who had been looking everywhere for Mowgli, arrived just in time! The bear grabbed Shere Khan by the tail and pulled him away from his friend. The vultures came back, picked up Mowgli and flew him to a tree.

Suddenly, a bolt of lightning struck nearby and started a small fire. Mowgli climbed down from the tree, grabbed a burning branch and sneaked up behind Shere Khan.

He tied the branch to Shere Khan's tail. The terrified tiger ran away, never to be seen again. Mowgli had saved the day!

Once again, Mowgli walked through the jungle with Baloo and Bagheera. All of a sudden, the Man-cub heard a new and beautiful sound. It was a girl from the Man-village, singing sweetly. When Mowgli tried to impress the girl, she smiled at him and began to head towards the village. Mowgli followed her and turned to wave goodbye to Baloo and Bagheera.

The bear and panther watched Mowgli leave. Their Man-cub had found his true home at last… but they knew he would never forget his jungle friends.

DISNEY

101
DALMATIANS

Once upon a time, two Dalmatians named Pongo and Perdita fell in love. Luckily, their owners, two humans named Roger and Anita, also fell in love. They all moved to a cosy house in London and soon fifteen puppies were born.

Just after the puppies arrived, an old school friend of Anita's dropped by. Her name was Cruella De Vil. She wore a large fur coat and her hair was half-black and half-white. She had heard about the puppies and wanted to buy them.

Roger and Anita weren't interested, but Cruella insisted. She even got out her chequebook. As Roger and Cruella argued, the woman shook her pen and splashed ink all over him.

"We're not selling the puppies… and that's final!" Roger yelled.

Pongo and Perdita were delighted with the puppies. One was so tiny, they didn't think he would make it. But somehow he survived. When his spots came in, they formed the shape of a horseshoe on his back, so he was named Lucky.

Another puppy had a black patch over his eye, so he was called Patch. One of their brothers was named Rolly, and they had a sister named Penny.

The puppies all liked to play together. Some nights, they even watched TV. They were a happy family.

One day, Roger and Anita took Pongo and Perdita for a walk. While they were out, Horace and Jasper, two of Cruella's henchmen, went to their house, pretending to be from the electric company. When the two men got inside, they locked Nanny, the housekeeper, in a room, put the puppies in a large bag, and left. Then, they drove out to Cruella's country estate and waited to hear from her.

When Nanny finally escaped, she saw that the puppy basket was empty and immediately called the police.

Soon Pongo and Perdita returned. They could not believe their eyes – their puppies had been stolen!

Pongo and Perdita knew that the Twilight Bark was their only hope. They got Roger and Anita to take them to a park, where they could bark the message to all the dogs in London. Those dogs would pass it along to the animals who lived in the country. Maybe one of them would have seen the puppies.

"Fifteen Dalmatian puppies stolen!" Pongo barked. A Great Dane heard his plea and spread the news. Before long, dogs all over England had heard about the stolen puppies.

Later that night, the Twilight Bark reached a quiet farm, where a cat named Sergeant Tibs heard it.

He awakened the Colonel, an old English sheepdog, and told him about the dognapping.

Sergeant Tibs thought that he'd heard barking at the old De Vil house. He and the Colonel set out for the gloomy mansion.

The sheepdog and cat arrived at Cruella's house and Sergeant Tibs went inside. He discovered the missing Dalmatians, plus eighty-four others! There were ninety-nine puppies altogether!

He told the Colonel to use the Twilight Bark to pass along the news that the pups had been located.

When Pongo and Perdita heard, they set off for the countryside right away.

Meanwhile, Tibs and the Colonel kept a close watch over the puppies. Cruella soon arrived and they found out that she wanted to use the puppies to make fur coats!

"I don't care how you kill the little beasts, but do it. And do it now!" she told Jasper and Horace. After she left, the two men decided to finish watching TV before they did anything.

Luckily, Tibs had heard the whole thing. He came up with a plan to help the pups escape through a hole in the wall. The cat led the Dalmatians down the stairs and hid them under the staircase. They were trembling with fear.

Jasper and Horace realised the pups were gone and started to search for them. Just as they found the puppies, Pongo and Perdita arrived and attacked the two bad men.

The puppies ran outside to safety. Perdita and Pongo soon followed, having momentarily foiled Horace and Jasper.

Their fifteen puppies called out to them. "Mum! Dad! I sure missed you. Here we are!"

"Oh, my darlings. My darlings!" Perdita gushed, thankful to be reunited with her children.

When Pongo and Perdita learnt about Cruella's plans for the other Dalmatians, they decided to take all ninety-nine puppies back to London. They would have to be careful, though, for they knew Cruella and her men would be searching for them.

The Dalmatians thanked the Colonel and Tibs for their help and started walking through the snow towards home. When the dogs realised Jasper and Horace were following them, they walked on the frozen river so they didn't leave any tracks. Soon, they heard a van coming and hid under a bridge.

The van stopped and Horace got out. "What if they went down the froze-up creek so's not to leave their tracks?" he asked Jasper.

"Dogs ain't that smart," Jasper replied. Horace got back in the van and the two drove off.

The dogs started walking down the frozen creek again. But it was a long journey. Before long, the puppies were exhausted and hungry. After a while, Lucky couldn't walk anymore, so his father carried him.

Thankfully, a collie soon met them and led them to a dairy farm. The puppies rested in the hay for a while and drank some milk.

The food made the puppies strong enough to continue to a town called Dinsford, where a Labrador brought them to a blacksmith's shop to rest. Later, they would board a van that was bound for London.

While they were waiting, Cruella arrived. Pongo knew that the puppies couldn't walk right by her to get on the van. But they were too small to travel the rest of the way on foot.

Lucky and Patch got in a fight while their father tried to come up with a plan. As they tussled, the puppies rolled round in the ashes of the fireplace. Soon, they were black with soot. Pongo glanced over at them and came up with an idea – all the puppies should cover themselves in ashes. That way, Cruella wouldn't recognise them.

"Come on kids, roll in the soot!" he cried, and the puppies rolled round until their fur was completely covered.

Since the pups were disguised, Pongo and Perdita thought it was safe to board the van. They walked right past Cruella. But just as the last group of puppies was about to hop on, a clump of snow fell and washed the soot off one of them.

From her car, Cruella could see it was a Dalmatian.

"Jasper! Horace!" she yelled to her men, who had arrived in Dinsford in their own car. "There they go! After them!"

The van with the puppies in took off and Cruella zoomed after it. She tried to run it off the road, even driving through a barricade. But while Cruella was chasing the van, Jasper and Horace were coming at it from a different direction.

They didn't see her car. The van avoided both cars, but Cruella, Jasper and Horace crashed into each other.

Cruella's fancy car was ruined. There was no way she'd be able to get the puppies now.

Pongo, Perdita and all ninety-nine puppies arrived back in London safely and hurried home.

Roger and Anita were surprised to see so many puppies. They cleaned the soot off them and began to count. With Pongo and Perdita, there were 101 Dalmatians!

"What'll we do with them?" Anita asked.

"We'll keep them," Roger answered. "We'll buy a big place in the country, and we'll have a plantation," he said. "A Dalmatian plantation!"

And that's exactly what they did.

One December evening, a businessman named Jim hurried home through the snow. He was very excited about the Christmas present he'd just picked for his wife.

When Jim arrived, he presented the gift. "It's for you, Darling."

"Oh Jim, dear," said his wife. Before she could open the box, the lid came off all by itself, revealing an adorable cocker spaniel.

The puppy looked up at the happy couple. "You like her, Darling?" Jim asked.

"What a perfectly beautiful little lady," his wife replied.

So, the puppy came to know her new family as Jim Dear and Darling. And they decided to name her Lady.

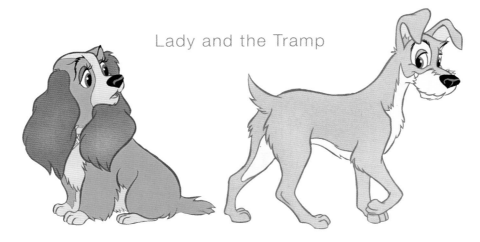

By summer, Lady enjoyed going for afternoon walks with Darling. But one day, no matter how much Lady begged, her owner would not go outside. Lady soon learned that Darling was expecting a baby.

In the yard, Lady told her good friends Jock, a Scottish terrier, and Trusty, a bloodhound, the news.

At that moment, a scruffy dog named Tramp wandered down the street. Tramp had no home and did not know what it was like to belong to a loving family. He'd overheard what Lady had said to others.

"When a baby moves in, the dog moves out," he told her.

Jock growled. Tramp moved on, but Lady thought about what he'd said.

Soon the baby arrived and Lady had one more wonderful person to care for and love.

She decided that Tramp had been wrong.

Several weeks later, Lady noticed that Jim Dear and Darling had packed their bags. "Don't worry, old girl," Jim told Lady. "We'll be back in a few days."

"And Aunt Sarah will be here," Darling added.

"With you here to help her—" Jim began.

Just then, the doorbell rang. It was Aunt Sarah and she'd brought her cats, Si and Am. After Jim Dear and Darling left, the cats began to act up. They attacked the canary and the goldfish, then ruined Darling's pretty living room. Lady tried to stop them, but Si and Am made it look like she had attacked them and made the mess.

Aunt Sarah was very angry with Lady. She took her to the pet shop and told the assistant, "I want a muzzle. A good, strong muzzle."

Aunt Sarah held Lady down, while the assistant fastened a muzzle around her head. But it was more than Lady could bear. After all, she hadn't done anything wrong.

So, she yanked her lead from Aunt Sarah's hands and ran away as fast as she could.

When Lady stopped to catch her breath, she realised she was in a strange part of town. A pack of mean dogs surrounded her.

Just then, Tramp appeared. He saw that Lady was in danger. He bravely fought the stray dogs, finally chasing them away.

"Ya poor kid!" said Tramp. He took Lady to the zoo, where a friendly beaver chewed through the muzzle strap.

That night, Tramp took Lady to one of his favourite spots – Tony's Restaurant. "The very place for a very special occasion," said Tramp.

Tony, the owner, served the meal. "The best spaghetti in town," he said. By candlelight, the two dogs shared the delicious pasta. Tony sang to them while they ate. Lady and Tramp did not even notice that they were eating the same long piece of spaghetti until they reached the middle and their lips met in a kiss!

Later, Lady and Tramp fell asleep in the park. The next morning, they woke up when a rooster crowed. "I should have been home hours ago," Lady said.

Tramp did not believe in having to do anything or having to be anywhere. He did not understand why Lady would want to leave.

"Open your eyes to what a dog's life can really be!" Tramp told Lady. "Ever chase chickens?" he asked, as he rushed into a pen filled with the squawking birds.

"We shouldn't!" Lady cried. She started to follow Tramp, but a net suddenly surrounded her. A dogcatcher put her in a van and drove her to the pound.

The dogs at the pound began to tease Lady. She was afraid and very upset.

Peg, a fluffy Pekingese, came to her rescue. "Can't you see the poor kid's scared enough?" she asked.

Lady was relieved when Aunt Sarah arrived to pick her up.

Aunt Sarah brought Lady home and chained her to the kennel in the back garden. Soon, Tramp came to apologise. "I thought you were right behind me. Honest!" he said. But Lady was too upset to listen. She was embarrassed that she had been locked up and she blamed him.

As Tramp left, Lady saw a rat scurry up a vine to the baby's room. Lady chased after it, but she was stopped by her chain. She barked as loudly as she could. Aunt Sarah stuck her head out the window. "Stop that racket!" she yelled.

Tramp came running. "What's wrong?" he asked.

"A rat!" Lady cried. "Upstairs in the baby's room!"

Tramp ran inside the house. Lady pulled at her chain until it broke, then rushed upstairs to help fight the rat.

Tramp accidentally knocked over the cot, as he raced after the rodent. Luckily, the baby was fine. Lady rushed in and watched over the baby while Tramp fought the rat behind the curtains. Finally, Tramp emerged and limped towards Lady, licking his paw.

Aunt Sarah came to the nursery and saw Lady and Tramp standing by the baby. "You vicious brutes!" she cried. Then she called the pound to take Tramp away. She hadn't noticed the dead rat by the curtains.

The dogcatcher arrived and loaded Tramp into his waggon. Just then, Jim Dear and Darling came home. "What's going on here?" Jim wondered.

Lady led Jim Dear to the nursery and he lifted the curtains.

"A rat!" Aunt Sarah shrieked.

Outside the house, Trusty and Jock overheard Aunt Sarah scream. They realised that Tramp had been misjudged. "We've got to stop that waggon!" Trusty exclaimed.

They soon caught up with the dogcatcher. Trusty barked very loudly. The horses got spooked and reared. The waggon tipped over – right onto poor Trusty!

Then, Jim Dear and Lady arrived in a taxi.

Lady found Tramp in the back of the overturned waggon, and they happily touched noses.

Then Lady saw Trusty lying in the snow.

She hurried over. He had a broken leg, but he would be all right.

By the time Christmas arrived, Trusty was doing just fine. His leg was bandaged, but he was able to walk over with Jock to visit Lady and her new family.

Jim Dear and Darling had been so grateful to Tramp for saving the baby that they asked him to live with them. Lady and Tramp had four adorable puppies and they had never been happier.

They knew how lucky they were to have such a nice home – and such a wonderful family to share it with.

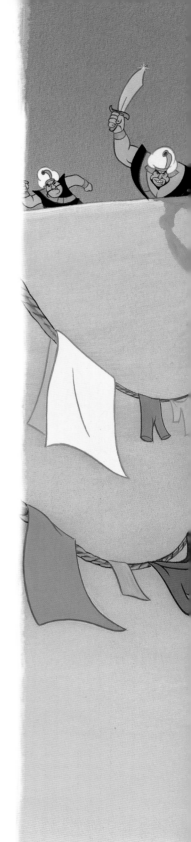

Long ago, in a faraway land called Agrabah, there lived a poor orphan named Aladdin. One day in the market, he stole some bread for his dinner. The Sultan's guards chased him, but he and his pet monkey, Abu, escaped. Just as Aladdin was about to eat, he noticed two children who looked hungrier than he was, so he gave the bread to them.

"Things will change," he promised Abu. "Someday we'll be rich and never have any problems at all!"

That afternoon at the palace, the Sultan reminded his daughter, Princess Jasmine, that the laws of the kingdom stated she must marry a prince before her next birthday. She had just three days left. She hadn't liked any of the suitors who had proposed to her. They had only been interested in wealth and power.

Jasmine decided she would rather leave the palace than marry someone she didn't love. She disguised herself in an old peasant robe and said goodbye to her pet tiger, Rajah.

Soon, Jasmine arrived at the market. She took an apple and gave it to a child who had no money. When Jasmine could not pay for the fruit, the angry merchant called the guards. Aladdin came to her rescue and the two escaped.

When Aladdin and Jasmine were far enough away, they stopped and talked about their lives. They realised they had a lot in common.

Suddenly the guards found them. They released the princess but took Aladdin to the Sultan's dungeon. Aladdin realised he had fallen in love with Jasmine, even before the guards had revealed she was a princess. But he knew she would never love him in return, for he was very poor.

Meanwhile, the Sultan's evil adviser, Jafar, had heard of a special lamp – one that would give him great power. The lamp was in the Cave of Wonders.

According to legend, only a person who was a diamond in the rough could enter the cave and come out alive. Jafar knew Aladdin had rescued the princess and thought he would be able to retrieve the lamp. He could also see how much the young man liked Jasmine.

Jafar disguised himself as an old prisoner and went into the dungeon. "Help me," he said to Aladdin. "There is a cave filled with treasure, enough to impress even your princess." In exchange, all Jafar wanted was for Aladdin to bring him the lamp.

Aladdin agreed and Jafar showed him how to escape from the dungeon.

Aladdin and Abu went into the cave. A flying carpet appeared and led them to the lamp. As Aladdin reached for it, Abu grabbed a large, sparkling jewel.

The cave began to collapse and the opening closed. Aladdin and Abu were safe, but trapped.

"This lamp looks worthless," Aladdin said. He rubbed the dusty lamp and an enormous genie appeared.

"Master," the Genie said, "I can grant you three wishes."

Aladdin tricked the Genie into getting them out of the cave. Then, he used his first wish to become a prince so Jasmine would want to marry him. He promised to use his last wish to set the Genie free.

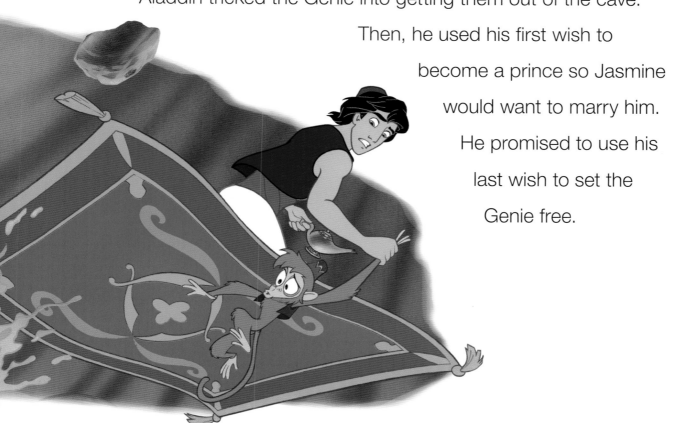

Later that day, Aladdin arrived at the palace in grand style, introducing himself as Prince Ali Ababwa. But Jasmine was not impressed. That evening, Aladdin, as Prince Ali, invited her for a ride on the Magic Carpet. Jasmine thought that the prince looked very familiar. "You remind me of someone I met in the marketplace," she said.

"I have servants who go to the marketplace," Aladdin lied. "So, it couldn't have been me you met." But when Jasmine took his hand to step aboard the carpet, she knew she could trust him.

The Magic Carpet took them on a tour of the city and beyond, then back to the palace. "That was just wonderful," Jasmine said with a sigh. Somewhere along the way she had fallen in love.

Aladdin was thrilled that things finally seemed to be going his way.

But just then, the Sultan's guards appeared and seized the young man. Under orders from Jafar, they tossed him into the sea. Aladdin summoned the Genie and used his second wish to save his own life.

Aladdin returned to the palace to confront Jafar and reveal his true identity to the princess. But before he got a chance, Iago, Jafar's parrot, stole the magic lamp and Jafar became the Genie's new master.

"I wish to rule on high as sultan!" Jafar commanded.

The Genie was forced to obey. He lifted the palace out of the ground and placed it atop a mountain.

"You will bow to me!" Jafar ordered the princess and her father. Jasmine refused. So Jafar used his second wish to become the world's most powerful sorcerer.

Jafar changed Aladdin back into a beggar and sent him far away to a snowy wasteland. Aladdin knew he had to defeat Jafar. Luckily, he found the Magic Carpet buried in the snow and they quickly flew back to Agrabah.

Jafar was furious when Aladdin returned. He put Jasmine inside an hourglass that was filling with sand. Then, he trapped Aladdin in a ring of swords. But the young man pulled one of the swords from the ground and challenged Jafar, who transformed into a giant snake.

Aladdin fought to free Jasmine, but Jafar caught him in his snake coils.

"Without the Genie, boy," the evil man hissed, "you're nothing!"

Aladdin thought of a way to trick Jafar. "The Genie has more power than you'll ever have!" he cried.

So Jafar used his third wish to become a genie. But he forgot that genies can only come out of their lamps to serve others. Jafar soon disappeared into a glowing black lamp.

Aladdin broke the hourglass and caught Jasmine in his arms just before the sand completely covered her. Then, the Genie threw Jafar's lamp far away.

Aladdin still had one wish left. Instead of asking to become a prince again, he wished for the Genie's freedom. Then, he told Jasmine who he really was.

The Sultan decided to change the law so that the princess could marry whoever she thought was worthy.

Jasmine ran into Aladdin's arms. "I choose you, Aladdin," she said, tenderly. And they lived happily ever after.

Long ago, there lived a man named Geppetto who carved music boxes and clocks. One day, he made a special puppet and named it Pinocchio. That night, Geppetto saw a star in the sky and made a wish. Then, he turned to his cat, Figaro, and told him, "I wished that my little Pinocchio might be a real boy!"

After Geppetto had gone to sleep, the Blue Fairy came to his workshop. "Good Geppetto," she said, "you give so much happiness to others – you deserve to have your wish come true."

The Blue Fairy touched the puppet gently with her wand. "Little puppet made of pine, wake! The gift of life be thine!" And in the blink of an eye, Pinocchio came to life.

"I can walk!" he cried. "Am I a real boy?"

"No, Pinocchio," the Blue Fairy replied. "To make Geppetto's wish come true will be entirely up to you. Prove yourself brave, truthful and unselfish."

The Blue Fairy decided to ask Jiminy Cricket to help Pinocchio. Jiminy Cricket was a small cricket who travelled from house to house looking for a warm place to stay and sing. He wore a suit and carried an umbrella. And that night, he was staying in Geppetto's workshop.

The Blue Fairy touched Jiminy Cricket with her magic wand. With that, he became Pinocchio's conscience, a voice of reason that would help the puppet know right from wrong.

As the Blue Fairy left, she said, "Now remember, Pinocchio, be a good boy and always let your conscience be your guide."

Later that night, Geppetto woke to find his precious wooden puppet alive.

He grabbed Pinocchio and swung him in the air. "It's my wish!" he cried. "It's come true!"

He proudly introduced his little wooden boy to Figaro and to his goldfish, Cleo. After some celebrating, they all went back to sleep.

The next morning, Geppetto gave Pinocchio an apple and a book and sent him to school. "Goodbye, son!" he called. "Hurry back!"

Pinocchio set off without Jiminy Cricket, who had overslept. Along the way, a fox named Honest John asked Pinocchio to be in a show at the theatre. The fox told him he would be famous and didn't need to go to school.

Jiminy caught up with Pinocchio and tried to stop him, but the puppet had already decided to be in the show.

That night, Pinocchio had great fun as he danced on the stage. The audience loved him and Stromboli, the man who put on the show, was very excited. But when Pinocchio tried to go home, Stromboli locked him in a cage.

Jiminy Cricket tried to open the cage, but he couldn't. Pinocchio began to sob. "I guess I'll never see my father again," he said, sadly.

Then, the Blue Fairy appeared. She asked Pinocchio why he hadn't gone to school. He lied and told her he had met some monsters. Suddenly, his nose began to grow. Every time he lied, his nose grew a little longer! It grew so long, leaves began to grow on it, like they would on a tree branch. Finally, a nest with some birds appeared on the end of it.

"Perhaps you haven't been telling the truth," the Blue Fairy remarked. "You see, Pinocchio, a lie keeps growing and growing until it's as plain as the nose on your face."

Pinocchio promised the Blue Fairy that he would never lie again. She returned his nose to its normal size and unlocked the cage.

Pinocchio and Jiminy Cricket got away from there as quickly as they could.

Pinocchio was on his way home when he ran into Honest John again. The evil fox convinced him to go to a place called Pleasure Island. So, Pinocchio jumped aboard a coach with lots of other boys.

"Don't go, Pinoke!" cried Jiminy Cricket, but it was too late.

On Pleasure Island, Pinocchio and the other boys ran wild and stuffed themselves with sweets. Jiminy tried to get him to leave so that he'd have a chance at becoming a real boy, but Pinocchio wanted to stay. His fun did not last long, though. He suddenly began to grow donkey ears and a tail! Pinocchio was frightened. He and Jiminy Cricket ran for their lives, away from Pleasure Island. Pinocchio wanted to see his father.

But when they got home, Geppetto was not there. Pinocchio was very upset and wondered where his father could be. Then a dove appeared with a note. It said that Geppetto had gone to sea to look for Pinocchio. His boat had been swallowed by a whale, but he was still alive.

Pinocchio set off at once to look for his father. He dived into the ocean and found him in the belly of a great whale. Geppetto was thrilled to see his son, but he didn't know how they would escape.

Then, Pinocchio had an idea – they would make the whale sneeze. Together, he and Geppetto built a fire. There was so much smoke that soon…

… ahhhhchooo! The whale sneezed. Father and son were thrown into the sea. Fighting the waves, Pinocchio got his father safely to shore. But the puppet was tired and Geppetto later found him facedown in the water.

He scooped Pinocchio up and carried him home. Geppetto thought his son was gone forever. He began to cry. But the Blue Fairy had seen how brave and unselfish Pinocchio had been, so she turned him into a boy.

Pinocchio opened his eyes and sat up. "I'm a real boy!" he cried, hugging his father. Geppetto's wish had come true, and father and son lived happily ever after.